22517

DATE DUE

Top 10 RUNNING BACKS

Chris W. Sehnert

ABDO & Daughters
Publishing

Published by Abdo & Daughters, 4940 Viking Drive, Suite 622, Edina, Minnesota 55435.

Copyright © 1997 by Abdo Consulting Group, Inc., Pentagon Tower, P.O. Box 36036, Minneapolis, Minnesota 55435 USA. International copyrights reserved in all countries. No part of this book may be reproduced in any form without written permission from the publisher.

Printed in the United States.

Cover and Interior Photo credits: Allsports Photos
                                 Wide World Photos
                                 Bettmann Photos
                                 Sports Illustrated

Edited by Paul Joseph

Library of Congress Cataloging-in-Publication Data

Sehnert, Chris W.
        Top 10 Running Backs/ by Chris W. Sehnert
                p   cm. -- (Top 10 Champions)
        Includes index.
        Summary: Covers the careers and statistics of ten NFL running backs:Emmitt
        Smith, Jim Brown, Jim Taylor, Larry Csonka, Franco Harris, Tony Dorsett, John
        Riggins, Walter Payton, Ottis Anderson, and Marcus Allen.
        ISBN 1-56239-792-3
        1. Running backs (football)--United States--Biography--Juvenile literature. 2.
        Running backs (football)--rating of--United States--Juvenile literature. [1.
        Football players.] I. Title. II. Series: Sehnert, Chris W.
        Top 10 Champions.
        GV939.A1S38   1997
        796.332'092'2--dc21   96-52409
        [B]   CIP
                                                                   AC

Table of Contents

Jim
BROWN

The history of the National Football League (NFL) is filled with the accomplishments of its star players. From Jim Thorpe to Emmitt Smith, many of the greatest athletes in football have played the position of running back. In the 1920s, Bronislaw "Bronco" Nagurski gained a reputation for carrying would-be tacklers on his back, as he rumbled towards the

end zone for another score. Perhaps the greatest running back of them all was Jim Brown. Combining the power of Nagurski with the overall athleticism of Thorpe, Jim Brown broke nearly every NFL rushing record on the books. After nine seasons with the Cleveland Browns, he left football for a career as a movie actor. He has since taken his place among the immortals of the game in the Professional Football Hall of Fame.

James Nathaniel Brown was born on St. Simon Island, Georgia. He was raised by his grandmother and great-grandmother until he was seven years old. He then moved to Manhasset, Long Island, New York, where he lived with his mother. Jim's father was a professional boxer, who had a brief fighting career. He left the family when Jim was a young child. At Manhasset Valley Elementary School, Plandome Road Junior High School, and the Manhasset Police Boys' Club, Jim began to develop his athletic prowess. He played football, basketball, baseball, and lacrosse with equal enthusiasm. By the age of 14, Jim was in the starting lineup for the Manhasset High School football team.

Jim had several opportunities to pick from when he graduated from high school. He was pursued by the New York Yankees and Boston (now Atlanta) Braves to play baseball, and was courted by 42 colleges and universities for athletic scholarships. He chose to attend Syracuse University on a football scholarship. Jim led the Syracuse football team to a high ranking on the national collegiate scene. He was an All-American in his senior season. On New Year's Day, 1957, he scored three touchdowns (TDs), as Syracuse lost (28-27) to Texas Christian University in the Cotton Bowl.

The Cleveland Browns chose Jim Brown in the first-round of the 1957 NFL Draft. He broke his first NFL record in his rookie season, rushing for 237 yards in a single game. The Browns were the NFL's Eastern Conference Champions that season, but lost to the Detroit Lions in the NFL Championship game. Jim was the league's leading rusher and was awarded the NFL's Rookie of the Year and Most Valuable Player (MVP) honors!

Jim Brown played professional football for nine seasons. He was the league's leading rusher eight times, a record that stands to this day. All told, Jim held 14 NFL records when he retired after the 1965 season. He was the league's all-time leading rusher, and had scored more TDs than anyone in the game's history. His brightest moment came at the conclusion of the 1964 season, as the Cleveland Browns defeated the Baltimore Colts in the NFL Championship Game. Jim Brown is a legend in the game of football. While his records continue to fall more than 30 years after his retirement, no running back, before or since, has dominated the game of football as well as he.

PROFILE:
Jim Brown
Born: February 17, 1936
Height: 6' 2"
Weight: 228 pounds
Position: Running Back
College: Syracuse University
Teams: Cleveland Browns (1957-1965)

CHAMPIONSHIP SEASONS

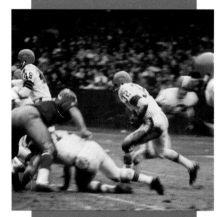

Fullback Jim Brown #32 carries the ball against the Washington Redskins, 1965.

**1964
NFL Championship**
Cleveland Browns (27)
vs. Baltimore Colts (0)

MAN FOR ALL SEASONS

Jim Brown was an outstanding all-around athlete. At Manhasset High School, he once scored 55 points in a basketball game. His abilities as a pitcher and first baseman drew the attention of the New York Yankees manager Casey Stengel. Jim's skill at the sport of lacrosse earned him All-American honors at Syracuse University. In total, he received ten varsity letters as a college athlete—three each in football and lacrosse, and two each in basketball and track. He passed-up an opportunity to represent the United States Olympic Team as a decathlon man saying later, "It wouldn't have been fair. I was in Syracuse on a football scholarship, and the Olympics would have cut into the time I was committed to give to football."

A Syracuse boxing promoter named Norman Rothschild was convinced Jim could be the heavyweight champion of the world. He offered him a $150,000 contract when he graduated from college. Jim chose to play football for the Cleveland Browns where he became one of the greatest running backs in the history of the NFL.

Jim Brown, halfback at Syracuse, 1957.

STILL STANDING

Most yards per rushing attempt, career	Jim Brown-5.22
Most years leading league in rushing yards	Jim Brown-8
Most consecutive years leading league in rushing yards	Jim Brown-5
Most seasons leading league in rushing attempts	Jim Brown-6
Most seasons leading league in combined yardage	Jim Brown-5
Most consecutive years leading league in combined yardage	Jim Brown-4

MADE TO BE BROKEN

JIM BROWN'S 14 NFL RECORDS AND THE MEN WHO CURRENTLY OWN THEM:

Jim Brown running for Cleveland.

Jim Brown	**Current Record Holder**
Most yards rushing, career-12,312	Walter Payton-16,726
Most yards rushing, season-1,863	Eric Dickerson-2,105
Most yards rushing, game-237 (twice)	Walter Payton-275
Most Touchdowns, career-126	Jerry Rice-156 (Thru 1995)
Most Touchdowns, season-21	Emmitt Smith-25
Most games 100 yards rushing, career-58	Walter Payton-77
Most seasons 1000 yards rushing, career-7	Walter Payton-10
Most combined yardage, career-15,459	Walter Payton-21,803

SILVER SCREEN

Jim Brown was only 29 years old when he retired from professional football. He had already shattered nearly every NFL record a running back could break. He made his big-screen debut in the post-Civil War film *Rio Conchos*, in 1964. He would later play a starring role in the World War II classic, *The Dirty Dozen*.

7

Jim
TAYLOR

Most running backs have a simple objective when carrying the football: Avoid Tacklers. This, however, was not the case when Jim Taylor carried the ball. Jim played fullback for the Green Bay Packers during four of their NFL Championship seasons in the 1960s. Describing his own unique philosophy of running he said, "football is a contact sport. You've got to punish the tacklers–deal out more misery than they deal out to you." No player has ever enjoyed a head-on collision as much as Jim Taylor. And, no running back has ever dealt-out more punishment.

James Charles Taylor was born in Baton Rouge, Louisiana. Life was never easy for Jim, and he grew strong in the face of it. His father was seriously disabled and died when Jim was nine years old. Jim's mother worked at a laundromat, but could scarcely provide food and shelter for herself and her son. At the age of ten, Jim began working and supporting himself. He delivered newspapers in the morning and the afternoon. He caddied at the local golf club and picked up odd jobs at construction sights. The money he made bought his clothing, but he paid the price with loneliness.

At Baton Rouge High School, Jim made the varsity basketball team as a freshman. He had developed his skill practicing by moonlight in a school yard, and occasionally breaking into school gyms at night. As a junior, he tried football for the first time. He began as a third-string fullback. Then in his senior year, Jim's star potential began to rise.

He became the first athlete ever chosen as a High School All-American in both football and basketball. In the 1954 High School All-American Football Game, Jim Taylor was the MVP.

Jim was widely recruited to play basketball by colleges and universities across the south. Deciding to stay close to home and play football, he chose Louisiana State University. Unfortunately, Jim's schoolwork was not as outstanding as his athletic ability, and he was forced to leave LSU in his sophomore year. In a twist of fate, Jim ended up at Hinds Junior College in Raymond, Mississippi, where he raised his grade point average and met his future wife. He returned to LSU for his junior year, and began to build his reputation as a ferocious fullback. "He'll kill you for a yard," said his opponents, and as a linebacker and place-kicker he was equally as deadly.

In 1958, Jim became a member of the Green Bay Packers. The team finished with the worst record (1-10) in football that season. Jim spent most of his time on the bench. Vince Lombardi took over the Packers' head coaching job in 1959. Lombardi installed Jim as his starting fullback that season, and Green Bay began to rise in the standings.

Jim rushed for over 1,000 yards five straight seasons, beginning in 1960. He was named the league's MVP in 1962, after leading Green Bay to its second straight NFL Championship. The Packers won three more NFL Championships between 1965 and 1967. Jim scored the first rushing TD in Super Bowl history. He went on to lead the Packers to the first-ever Super Bowl win when the NFL and AFL Champions met for the first time in 1967. The following season, Jim Taylor closed out his Hall-of-Fame career back home in Louisiana. He joined the New Orleans Saints for their first NFL season and his last.

PROFILE:
Jim Taylor
Born: September 20, 1935
Height: 6' 0"
Weight: 215 pounds
Position: Running Back
College: Louisiana State University
Teams: Green Bay Packers (1958-1966)
New Orleans Saints (1967)

CHAMPIONSHIP SEASONS

Jim Taylor (31).

1961
NFL Championship
Green Bay Packers (37) vs. New York Giants (0)

1962
NFL Championship
Green Bay Packers (16) vs. New York Giants (7)

1965
NFL Championship
Green Bay Packers (23) vs. Cleveland Browns (12)

1966
NFL Championship
Green Bay Packers (34) vs. Dallas Cowboys (27)

1966-67
Super Bowl I
Green Bay Packers (35) vs. Kansas City Chiefs (10)

HEAD BANGERS

In 1960, the Packers were defeated by the Philadelphia Eagles in the NFL Championship game (17-13). Chuck Bednarik was the Eagles' Hall-of-Fame linebacker, who became legendary for planting ball-carriers in their tracks. It was Bednarik who delivered Hall-of-Fame running back Frank Gifford to an early retirement.

On the final play of the 1960 NFL Championship game, Jim Taylor caught a pass from Bart Starr on the 8-yard line and was dropped by Bednarik preventing a game-winning score. Jim, who reportedly "enjoyed banging heads," had apparently met his match!

GOLDEN BACKFIELD

Jim was not the only Hall-of-Famer in the Green Bay Packers backfield of the 1960s. In fact, there were three. Along with quarterback Bart Starr was fellow inductee Paul Hornung. "The Golden Boy" was the Packers' halfback, and an outstanding ball-carrier in his own right. Hornung (1961), Taylor (1962), and Starr (1966) combined for three MVP Awards in a six year period!

Jim Taylor (31) runs through the Dallas Cowboys.

RUN TO DAYLIGHT

Vince Lombardi's famous philosophy for ball-carriers was "Run to Daylight." Jim Taylor did not always fully comply. In a game against the Chicago Bears, Jim broke through the first line of defense to find one man standing between he and the goal line. Rather than run past his opponent, Jim barreled right over him for the score. Later that week while watching films of the play, Lombardi stopped the projector to question his fullback. "You had a clear path, Jim," said Lombardi in amazement. "Why did you hit him?"

"Gotta sting 'em a little, coach," replied Jim with a laugh!

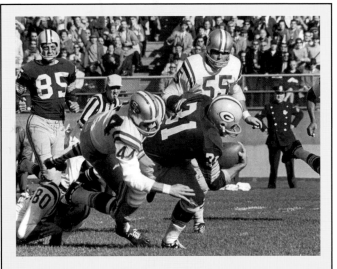

Jim Taylor (31) runs against the 49ers.

*T*AYLOR vs *B*ROWN

Jim Taylor had the unfortunate circumstance of sharing a similar career span with Jim Brown. Because of this fact, Taylor was often given second-billing when it came to naming the NFL's All-Pro Fullback. Brown was the league's leading rusher in eight of the nine seasons he played. In the one season he was not (1962), Jim Taylor led the league in rushing (1,474 yards), and was named the league's MVP.

Bill Austin, the Packers' offensive coordinator at the time, offered this comparison of the Hall-of-Fame fullbacks. "Brown is certainly more elusive. He won't let you grab a leg. Taylor will—and then he'll ram it through your chest!"

Larry CSONKA

Some running backs sprint past their opponents. Others use lightning quick cuts to avoid tacklers. Larry Csonka had a different way of gaining yards on the ground. He ran over and through defenders, as if bulldozing a path to the end zone. He was as tough a competitor as any that has ever played the game of football. He is probably the only player who has been penalized for unnecessary roughness—while carrying the football! In the early 1970s, he helped carry the Miami Dolphins to Super Bowl Championships in two straight seasons. Throughout his career Larry carried defenders upon his back, while grinding his way into the Professional Football Hall of Fame.

Lawrence Richard Csonka was raised on a farm in Stow, Ohio. He began building his power very early in life. "We worked 10 or 11 hours a day. When my father said we were going to build a barn in a month, we knew he really meant two weeks," Larry remembers. Larry's father was very strict, and not someone to be disobeyed. He worked days at the Goodyear Tire plant in Akron, Ohio, and often worked nights as a bouncer—throwing trouble makers out of local bars. Larry grew strong on the farm. At 12 years old, he was embarrassed to play little league baseball, since he was so much bigger than the other kids. Football became his sport of choice.

On the high school football field, Larry played nearly every position. He was most adept as a bone-crunching linebacker, and as an overpowering fullback. He was recruited by 50 colleges and universities to play football.

Larry's high school coach had played for Syracuse coach Ben Schwartzwalder, and persuaded him to accept a scholarship at Syracuse University.

Schwartzwalder's first impression was that Larry would make an outstanding college linebacker. Larry played the first three games of his sophomore season at that position, before being switched to offense. "Making him a linebacker was the biggest mistake I ever made," said Schwartzwalder. "I was lucky I changed my mind. I never saw such power and determination in a runner. He never stopped driving until he was on the ground." By his senior season, Larry had broken nearly every Syracuse rushing record, including those held by the legendary Jim Brown!

The Miami Dolphins made Larry their first round pick in the 1968 Draft. The Dolphins were a fairly new team, having joined the AFL (American Football League) through expansion only two years earlier. In 1970, Don Shula became the Dolphins' head coach. Through Shula's insistence, Larry cut his weight from 255 to 235 pounds. The Dolphins built their offense around their unstoppable fullback,

and soon became the best team in football. After suffering a defeat to the Dallas Cowboys in Super Bowl VI, the Dolphins returned the next year to record the only undefeated season in NFL history. For Larry, it was his second straight season of 1,000-yards rushing. He accomplished the feat for a third straight time in 1973, as the Dolphins were Super Bowl Champions once more.

Larry was named the MVP of Super Bowl VIII, rambling for 145 yards on 33 carries and scoring 2 TDs. In 1975, he left the Dolphins to join the Memphis Grizzlies of the soon to be defunct WFL (World Football League). He returned to play four more seasons in the NFL, before retiring as a member of the Miami Dolphins after the 1979 season. A tougher competitor never played the game of football.

PROFILE:
Larry Csonka
Born: December 25, 1946
Height: 6' 3"
Weight: 235 pounds
Position: Running Back
College: Syracuse University
Teams: Miami Dolphins (1968-1974, 1979), Memphis Grizzlies (1975), New York Giants (1976-1978)

PORTRAIT OF A CHAMPION

CHAMPIONSHIP
SEASONS

Larry Csonka (C) receives award for ECAC Player of the Year.

1972-73
Super Bowl VII
Miami Dolphins (14) vs. Washington Redskins (7)

1973-74
Super Bowl VIII
Miami Dolphins (24) vs. Minnesota Vikings (7)

HARD NOSE

Larry was raised to be a tough competitor. He and his brother shared a bedroom in the attic of their Ohio farmhouse. "It was so cold in the winter, I could watch my breath go the length of the room," he recalls. "I had a runny nose the first ten years of my life."

Once while attending his chores, he had his nose broken by a steer. The giant beast reared its head just as Larry was bending down to feed him. It was only the first of nine broken noses Larry would suffer. The last came in a football game against the Buffalo Bills. When he returned to the huddle, the blood gushing from his face made at least one teammate get sick. Larry smiled and continued playing.

Larry Csonka (39) runs through the Pitt defense while playing for Syracuse.

MOTHER KNOWS BEST

In college Larry constantly worked to build his strength. As a junior at Syracuse University, he admired the giant forearms of teammate Gary Bugenhagen, which were the biggest he'd ever seen. Bugenhagen told Larry he could build his forearms by banging them into things. The next summer, Larry returned to his family's farm to test the theory.

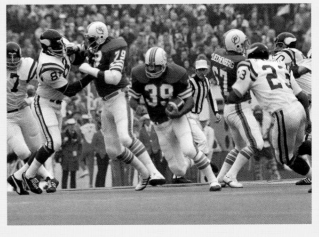

Larry Csonka running for Miami.

"My mother would raise hell," Larry remembered. "I used to leave a couple of hundred pounds of weights on my bed, and she couldn't lift them to straighten out the covers." Later that summer Larry's mother called coach Schwartzwalder to complain. "Get him out of here!" she shouted. "Make him come back to school early. He's too ready for football. He goes around the house all day slamming his forearms into walls! There's nothing but holes all over the house."

NICE GUY

Despite all of his notoriety for toughness, Larry wants to be known as a nice guy. "Hey, I like people," he exclaims. "Some people think I'm a brute, with my knuckles dragging on the ground. I don't like the image of me as a bulldozer or a battering ram. It reflects a certain type of mentality. I'm not some red-eyed monster with a forked tail rising out of the swamp."

Try telling that to the bear who met Larry on a hunting trip in Canada. While Larry lay sleeping, the wild animal crept up to investigate his camp. Reportedly, the bear started nibbling at him when Larry woke up and jabbed his elbow into the bear's ribcage, sending it fleeing into the woods. Larry passes off the incident with typical modesty. "It was only a small bear," he says with a laugh!

Franco
HARRIS

The Pittsburgh Steelers and their fans suffered through four decades without a football championship of any kind. Art Rooney, the team's owner, twice saved the organization from bankruptcy by combining them with other NFL franchises. By the early 1970s, he had begun to assemble a ball-club for the ages. In 1972, the Steelers won their first division title before being defeated by the Miami Dolphins in the AFC Championship Game. Franco Harris was the AFC's Rookie of the Year that season after becoming only the fifth player in NFL history to rush for 1,000-yards in his first season. Two years later, Franco was named MVP of Super Bowl IX, as the Steelers won the first of four NFL Championships.

Franco Harris was born at Fort Dix, New Jersey. He was the third of nine children born to Gina and Cadillac Harris. Franco's mother was from Pietro Sanca Lucca, Italy, where she met Cad, an American soldier, during World War II. When Franco was in junior high, his mother refused to allow him to play football. "She didn't understand the game. That's why she didn't want me to play," Franco said later. At Rancocas Valley Regional High School in Mount Holly, New Jersey, Franco's football legend began. He was a high school All-American at the position of running back.

Franco was recruited by Pennsylvania State University, where he played under head coach Joe Paterno. The Nitany Lions were a college football powerhouse in those years, led by another future NFL running back named Lydell Mitchell.

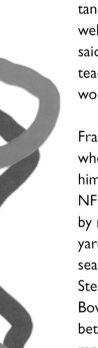

"I was used a whole lot for blocking," Franco recalls. "Mitchell deserved everything he got and more. Personally, I didn't feel I was playing second fiddle to him." Penn State scored victories in the 1969 Orange Bowl and the 1971 Cotton Bowl with their superstar backfield tandem. "Penn State prepared you well to come to the pros," Franco said, "and coach Paterno is a great teacher of discipline and hard work."

Franco's hard work was rewarded when the Pittsburgh Steelers made him a first round pick in the 1972 NFL Draft. He returned the favor by rushing for more than 1,000-yards eight times over the next 12 seasons. In the meantime, the Steelers won back-to-back Super Bowl Championships twice between 1974 and 1979. Franco ran like a bull coming out of the backfield. "You don't arm-tackle the man," Hall-of-Fame teammate Mel Blount recounted. "You've got to put some pad on him, and he punishes those guys." Franco punished the Minnesota Vikings in Super Bowl IX, piling up 158 yards on the ground. With four Super Bowl appearances, he remains among the all-time leaders for rushing yardage (354), and TDs (4). Franco Harris was an integral part of the Pittsburgh Steelers football dynasty of the 1970s. He retired after the 1984 season, and returned to a life-style outside of the NFL's limelight. Jack Ham, the Steelers' great linebacker later said, "I knew him when Penn State was recruiting him, and he has never changed. I think that's the thing I admire about him most: that despite all the publicity and all of the good things that have happened to him, he has never changed." Today, the careers of Franco Harris and his Steeler teammates Jack Ham, Mel Blount, Terry Bradshaw, Joe Greene, and Jack Lambert have been immortalized in the Professional Football Hall of Fame, along with Head Coach Chuck Noll and legendary owner Art Rooney.

PROFILE:
Franco Harris
Born: March 7, 1950
Height: 6' 2"
Weight: 225 pounds
Position: Running Back
College: Pennsylvania State University
Teams: Pittsburgh Steelers (1972-1983), Seattle Seahawks (1984)

CHAMPIONSHIP
SEASONS

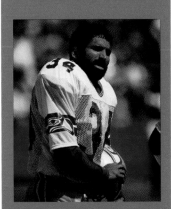

*Franco Harris
with Seattle.*

1974-75
Super Bowl IX
Pittsburgh Steelers (16)
vs. Minnesota Vikings (6)

1975-76
Super Bowl X
Pittsburgh Steelers (21)
vs. Dallas Cowboys (17)

1978-79
Super Bowl XIII
Pittsburgh Steelers (35)
vs. Dallas Cowboys (31)

1979-80
Super Bowl XIV
Pittsburgh Steelers (31)
vs. Los Angeles Rams (19)

IMMACULATE RECEPTION

The situation appeared hopeless for the Pittsburgh Steelers. Thirteen seconds remained in the first playoff game of their 40 year history (1972). The Steelers were trailing the Oakland Raiders (7-6), and with fourth down and ten yards to go, were down to their final play. Quarterback Terry Bradshaw faded back to pass and threw the ball deep downfield before being buried by the Raider defense. The ball was intended to find Pittsburgh's halfback Frenchy Fuqua, but ricocheted off Raider defensive back Jack Tatum. The deflected pass traveled halfway across the field where a surprised Franco Harris scooped it off his shoe-tops, before allowing it to reach the turf. Pittsburgh's star rookie kept his feet and rambled 42 yards for the winning TD!

Back home in New Jersey, Franco's mother was completing her holiday preparations. "Just before it happened I was outside, putting up a Christmas statue, the Blessing of the Three Kings," she recalls. "My three boys were inside watching the game on TV. They were too quiet. They weren't yelling. I knew things were bad. I knew I had to do something. I went inside and put on my favorite record. Beniamino Gigli singing 'Ave Maria.' Just then Franco made that catch and they won the game!"

The Steelers eventually lost to the Miami Dolphins in the 1972 AFC Championship game. Franco's miraculous effort in the previous game, however, will forever be remembered by the Pittsburgh faithful. The amazing play is known in the NFL history books as the "Immaculate Reception!"

FRANCO'S ITALIAN ARMY

Fans of the Pittsburgh Steelers had witnessed more than their share of defeat by the early 1970s. A town of blue-collar steelworkers, Pittsburgh, Pennsylvania, was hit hard by economic recession at the time their football team rose to prominence. Suddenly, Art Rooney's "lovable losers" became a team of great destiny. The city of Pittsburgh rallied around them in a display of togetherness not often witnessed in professional sports.

Franco Harris running past Browns defender.

Upon their heroes, Steeler fans bestowed nicknames that gave the team its identity. Their powerful defense became known as the "Steel Curtain," while Franco Harris had his own legion of followers. They took their nickname from Harris' ethnic descent, calling themselves, "Franco's Italian Army."

Franco Harris running against the Vikings.

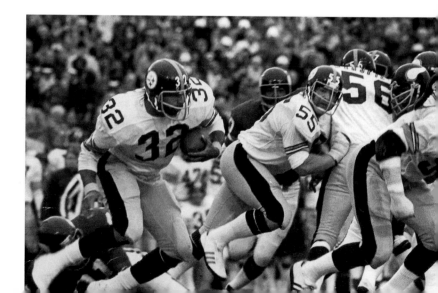

Tony DORSETT

To accelerate is to cause something to happen quicker than expected. In football, acceleration is a quality that allows a ball-carrier to elude tacklers. When a running back reaches the hole created by his blockers quicker than expected, he is more likely to break through to the open field. When Tony Dorsett found the open field there were few defenders capable of stopping his progress.

Tony was quite often the smallest player on the football field. To opposing defenses, he was always among the most dangerous. He could accelerate to a blazing top speed in a heartbeat, and stop just as quickly. Tony didn't run over tacklers—he bounced off them. With catlike grace, he would leap, spin, somersault, land on his feet, and continue downfield. Tony Dorsett is the all-time leading rusher in the history of college football. In the history of the NFL, he ranks third.

Anthony Drew Dorsett was born in Aliquippa, Pennsylvania. He was the sixth of seven children born to Myrtle and Westley Dorsett. Tony's father worked in the steel mills of Aliquippa. It was a fate Tony worked hard to avoid. "Mom instilled in me a lot of values that are still here," he remembers, "like respecting others and getting a first-rate education." As a junior high school student, he was elected to the National Honor Society.

At the age of 12, Tony was told he was too small to play football on the local "midget" league football team. The early rejection motivated him to become the best athlete he could be. He developed his strength and speed to compensate for his small size. He also

learned to be aggressive, a trait which caused him to be put on probation from his high school basketball team.

As a sophomore at Hopewell High School, Tony played outside linebacker for the football team. This time his aggressiveness combined with impressive speed led to some ferocious tackles. The next season, he took over at running back, and led Hopewell to the Midwestern Athletic Conference Championship. As a senior, Tony scored 23 TDs, and was named to the first-string High School All-American Team.

Tony attended the University of Pittsburgh where his football coach Johnny Majors said he became "like a man possessed in his dedication." With a daily ritual of weight training he added over 30 pounds to his slender physique. In his first season, he began transforming the Pitt Panthers into a winning ball club. Tony's 1,586-yards rushing that season was a new record for college freshman, landing him on the first of four straight College All-American Teams. As a senior, Tony led Pitt to an undefeated season, a victory in the Sugar Bowl, and the

1976 National Championship. At season's end, he was awarded the Heisman Trophy, as college football's most outstanding player. He also had accumulated 13 NCAA rushing records!

The Dallas Cowboys selected Tony as the second player taken overall in the 1977 NFL Draft. His impact was felt immediately as he rushed for over 1,000-yards in his rookie season. Tony was named the NFL's Rookie of the Year, and the Dallas Cowboys were the NFL Champions after defeating the Denver Broncos in Super Bowl XII. Tony Dorsett played 11 seasons with the Cowboys, surpassing the 1,000-yard rushing mark eight times. He became a member of the Professional Football Hall of Fame in 1994.

PROFILE:
Tony Dorsett
Born: April 7, 1954
Height: 5' 11"
Weight: 184 pounds
Position: Running Back
College: University of Pittsburgh
Teams: Dallas Cowboys (1977-1987), Denver Broncos (1988)

CHAMPIONSHIP
SEASONS

Tony Dorsett (33) running hard for the Pitt Panthers.

1977-78
Super Bowl XII
Dallas Cowboys (27) vs. Denver Broncos (10)

CAN'T TOUCH THIS

Tony Dorsett holds the NFL record for the longest run from the line of scrimmage. During a Monday Night Football game, on January 3, 1983, the Dallas Cowboys were backed-up on their own one-yard line. The Minnesota Vikings' defense was looking to record a safety, when Dallas handed the ball off to Tony on a run up the middle. With a burst of acceleration, he blew through the first line of defense and into the open field. By the time he reached the 20-yard line, it was apparent that no one would catch him. Tony's 99-yard TD scamper is one record that cannot be beat. Aside from that, replays showed Dallas had only ten men (one man short) on the field when the record rush took place!

IN THE BOOKS

NCAA Division I-A all-time leaders:
Most Yards Rushing/ Career: Tony Dorsett (6,082)

NFL all-time leaders:
Most Yards Rushing/ Career:
Walter Payton (16,726)
Eric Dickerson (13,259)
Tony Dorsett (12,739)

TROPHY CASE

1972–High School All-American Running Back
1973–NCAA All-American
   Running Back
1974–NCAA All-American
   Running Back
1975–NCAA All-American
   Running Back
1976–NCAA All-American
   Running Back
1976–Heisman Trophy
1976–Maxwell Award,
   outstanding college
   football player
1977–NFC Rookie of the
   Year
1981–NFC Player of the Year
1994–Elected to Professional
   Football Hall of Fame

Tony Dorsett with the Heisman Trophy.

*I*RISH EYES AREN'T SMILING

As a freshman running back for the Pittsburgh Panthers, Tony rushed for 209 yards in a game against Notre Dame. It was the most yardage the Fighting Irish had ever allowed a single running back. Two years later, Tony drew the Irish's ire once more. He broke his own record with a 303-yard performance!

Tony Dorsett (33) running for the Dallas Cowboys.

John RIGGINS

Conformity is acting or behaving by current customs or styles. It is to stay within the lines, to follow instructions even when you believe there is a better way. As a boy growing up in the tiny town of Centralia, Kansas, John Riggins learned to respect authority. He soon found out that blind faith was not always the wisest choice.

While preparing for a long-jump in a seventh grade track meet, John noticed the landing-pit seemed a bit too short. "I told the official, 'Look, the back of the pit's too close. Let me use the high school pit,'" he recalls. The official responded, "Nah, nah, you'll have no problem." John made the jump, cleared the pit, landed on the track, and separated the cartilage from his ankle. It was a defining moment in the life of one of the NFL's all-time greatest running backs.

John Riggins was the second of three sons born to Franklin and Mildred Riggins. "My dad had been a fullback at Wichita State in the 1930s," John said. "Sports were always very big in our family." John also excelled in his schoolwork, earning high grades and honorable mention in the state of Kansas'

seventh grade mathematics contest. "In Sunday school they said he was a disruptive influence at times, yet when they called on him he'd always come up with the answer," his mother recalls. "I liked to have fun," John responds, "and I found that nothing was more fun than going against the grain."

In Athletics, John was always pushed to a higher level of performance by his older brother Frank, Jr. As a sophomore at Centralia High School, John was a 185-pound halfback, while "Junior" was the senior quarterback. The next season, John took over behind the center, and was named to the All-State Team. As a senior, John was simply unstoppable. He was not only the fastest player on the field, but at 215 pounds, was quite often the biggest. Centralia outscored their opponents 457 to 24 that season, and John was rated as the top high school player in the nation. John followed his brother Junior to Kansas University, where they again shared the backfield in John's sophomore year. That season the Jayhawks went 9-1, losing to Penn State in the Orange Bowl. John led the Big Eight Conference in rushing his senior season, and was named to the College All-American Team. He majored in journalism and began to develop his reputation as a funky dresser. "He'd dress in overalls and carry a lunch pail and wear these little bitty wire-rim granny glasses," one acquaintance remembers.

The New York Jets made John the first running back selected in the 1971 NFL Draft. There, he joined a team that was soon to be past its prime, led by veteran quarterback Joe Namath. John was consistently voted the team's MVP during his five years with New York, and his flair for eccentricity flourished. He gained national exposure, not only for his tremendous athletic ability, but for his mohawk hairstyle and toenails, which he painted green. Feeling overly expended and under compensated, John determined to move on after the 1975 season.

The Washington Redskins became John's new team. He worked hard to conform to the coaching styles of three new head coaches in a period of six years. Finally in 1982, with the Redskins poised for the playoffs, John decided to take matters into his own hands.

He entered the office of head coach, Joe Gibbs, and made a simple demand. "I want the ball," John said. "You what?" was the reply. "The ball, give me the ball, I want it," John repeated. Gibbs understood, and John got the ball, again and again. The result was a record setting post-season streak, in which John Riggins gained at least 100 yards rushing in four straight games. He was named MVP of Super Bowl XVII, as the Redskins defeated the Miami Dolphins. No one was happier than coach Gibbs that John had learned to question authority!

PROFILE:
John Riggins
Born: August 4, 1949
Height: 6' 2"
Weight: 240 pounds
Position: Running Back
College: University of Kansas
Teams: New York Jets (1971-1975), Washington Redskins (1976-1979, 1981-1985)

CHAMPIONSHIP
SEASONS

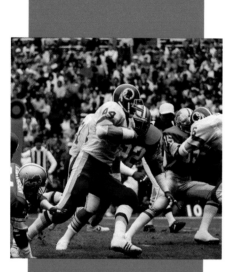

John Riggins running hard against the Detroit Lions.

1982-83
Super Bowl XVII
Washington Redskins (27)
vs. Miami Dolphins (17)

DIESEL AND THE HOGS

John Riggins ran with the football like a truck blowing through road blocks. For this reason, the Washington Redskins fans nicknamed him "Diesel," and tooted air horns each time he carried the ball. In 1982, the huge Redskins offensive line, who opened up the trucking lanes for Diesel, were nicknamed the "Hogs," making pig snouts fashionable attire at RFK stadium.

John Riggins while playing college ball at Kansas.

MY WAY

John was never a big fan of practicing. "My idea of a perfect practice would be to go out there and watch it for a while, have a few laughs and go in," he chuckles. On a more serious note he said, "I looked back on my career and it seemed to have followed a pattern. Every time I was told exactly what I was supposed to be doing and what the order of things should be...it blew up in my face. The other way, when I tried to do things my way, it seemed to work out better."

John Riggins carrying the ball, along with the Cowboys, into the end zone.

However he did it, John Riggins wound up his career as the sixth leading rusher in NFL history. He is now a member of the Professional Football Hall of Fame.

MOHAWK

In 1973, John's hairstyle drew lots of attention from the national media. In an interview with Paul Zimmermen of Sports Illustrated he explains why he did it. "Everyone who had long hair in those days was either a hippie or a war protester. I didn't see myself that way. So I shaved my head and grew a Mohawk. I was staking out my own territory, letting everyone around me know I was making my own decisions."

Walter PAYTON

How does one describe a running back who accumulated more combined yardage (21,803) than any player in NFL history? A man who completed his football career as the all-time leader in rushing attempts (3,838), rushing yards (16,726), and rushing TDs (110). A player who chalked up more 100-yard games (77) and more 1,000-yard seasons (10) than any who came before him. Walter Payton was not only the greatest running back in the long and storied history of the Chicago Bears, he also holds the team's all-time record for pass receptions. Add to that his value as an outstanding blocker, and his ability to throw TD passes. How do you describe such a man? Walter's fans and teammates did it with one word. *"SWEETNESS!"*

Walter Jerry Payton was the youngest of two sons born to Peter and Alyne Payton. As a boy growing up in Columbia, Mississippi, he enjoyed music and dancing more than anything else. While his older brother Eddie gained attention as an athlete, Walter played drums and sang in jazz-rock combos. Eddie became the star halfback for the Columbia High School football team. He would go on to play for Jackson State University, and later become a kick returner for the Minnesota Vikings. Before long, Walter would follow his brother's footsteps all the way to the NFL.

Walter's first excursion into sports was in track, where he set a local record for the long jump. After his brother had graduated, the Columbia High School football coach urged Walter to try out for the team. Though he was already a junior and had never played the game before, his impact was immediate. On his first carry he ran the ball 61 yards for a TD. To keep from tearing his uniform (and thereby upsetting his mother), Walter developed his technique of straight-arming defenders, before running over and past them. His overwhelming athletic ability drew widespread acclaim from the ranks of college recruiters.

Walter considered several offers from large Division I-A schools. In the end, he chose to stay close to home, joining his brother at the smaller Division I-AA, Jackson State. There, Walter eventually scored more points (464) than any player in NCAA (National Collegiate Athletic Association) history! He was used as both a punter and running back. He also developed his skill for throwing TD passes out of the halfback option play. He earned a Bachelor of Arts degree in Special Education in three and one-half years, and was now ready for a career in professional football.

The Chicago Bears made Walter their first selection in the 1975 NFL Draft. The Bears were the NFL's oldest franchise, but had not tasted post-season play since their 1963 NFL Championship. In his rookie season, Walter was the league's leading kickoff returner, but

Chicago finished with yet another dismal season record (4-10). In 1977, Walter emerged as the league's finest player, leading the Bears to their first playoff berth in 14 years. He won his second of five straight NFC rushing titles that season, set an NFL record for rushing yards in a single game (275), and became the youngest player ever to be named the league's MVP!

By 1985, the only thing missing from Walter Payton's incredible football resume was an NFL Championship. The crowning achievement came in Super Bowl XX, as the Bears defeated the New England Patriots. "Sweetness" retired after the 1987 season, and was inducted into the Professional Football Hall of Fame in 1993.

PROFILE:
Walter Payton
Born: July 25, 1954
Height: 5' 10"
Weight: 205 pounds
Position: Running Back
College: Jackson State University
Teams: Chicago Bears (1975-1987)

CHAMPIONSHIP SEASONS

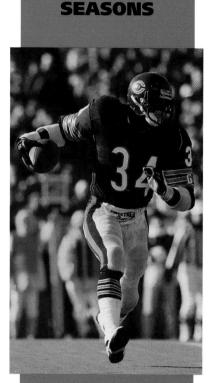

Bears' running back Walter Payton strides for the end zone.

1985-86
Super Bowl XX
Chicago Bears (46) vs. New England Patriots (10)

RECORD BOOK

NFL Records currently held by Walter Payton:

Most Career Rushing Yards: 16,726

Most years with 1,000 or more Rushing Yards: 10

Most Rushing Yards/ Single Game: 275

Most Games with 100 or more Rushing Yards/ Career: 77

Most Consecutive Games with 100 or more Rushing Yards/ Season: 9

Most Rushing Attempts/ Career: 3,838

Most Combined Net Yards/ Career: 21,803

Most Combined Attempts/ Career: 4,368

PAYTON AWARD

Each year since 1987 the most outstanding Division I-AA college football player has been honored for their achievements. The award is named for Walter Payton, whose outstanding professional career was preceded by his accomplishments at Jackson State University.

Walter Payton holding his Athlete of the Year trophy, 1985.

DESCRIPTIONS OF SWEETNESS

"Eddie was always running outside to practice things he'd seen in televised football games, but Walter never did that. He'd just sit and watch and that was all."
— Alyne Payton, Walter and Eddie's mother

Walter Payton makes a move.

"You really don't appreciate a Walter Payton until you are on the sidelines against him. We were hitting him with two and three men."
— Tom Landry, Dallas Cowboys Head Coach

"The guy's amazing. Week after week I see him put his head down and hit guys in the chest and *they* get carried off."
— Doug Plank, Walter's teammate with the Chicago Bears

"The first time I saw Walter Payton in the locker room I thought God must have taken a chisel and said, 'I'm gonna make me a halfback.'"
— Fred O'Connor, Chicago Bears coach

"You can't flow with the play because he'll cut back, and you can't tackle him below the waist because his legs are going all over the place. The best place to zero in is right at his belly button. But you don't try to punish him, because you'll miss him. You've got to grab him and get a firm hold."
— Jack Youngblood, Los Angeles Rams defensive end

"I guess my running style comes by instinct. I don't try to define it or explain it . . . only to improve it."   — Walter Payton

Sparetime

Walter enjoys fishing, hunting, golf, baseball, archery, dancing, and playing the drums. He lives with his wife Connie, whom he met in college, along with their son Jarret. He stays involved with many charities, especially benefiting retarded children and the deaf. Walter returned to Jackson State University after graduating, to further his Special Education degree and specialize in education for the hearing impaired.

Ottis ANDERSON

Football is a team sport. One man alone cannot make a team into a champion. Many of the NFL's greatest running backs have played their entire careers without the honor of being on a championship team. Eric Dickerson played 11 seasons and trails only Walter Payton on the all-time rushing list. He never appeared in a Super Bowl. Thurman Thomas has appeared in four NFL Championship games with the Buffalo Bills. He is among the all-time leaders for rushing yards and TDs in Super Bowl history, but he's never worn the ring of an NFL Champion.

In his first seven seasons, Ottis Anderson was consistently among the top running backs in professional football. He set an NFL rushing record (1,605 yards) for rookies in 1979, and rushed for over 1,000 yards five times in his first six seasons. His St. Louis Cardinals, however, were among the worst teams in football. When he was traded to the New York Giants midway through the 1986 season, he was relegated to short-yardage situations. The Giants were Super Bowl Champions that season, but Ottis played only a small role. He made a vow that if he ever returned to the "Big Dance," he would be the game's MVP. In Super Bowl XXV the Giants returned, and Ottis Anderson was true to his word.

Ottis Jerome Anderson was born in West Palm Beach, Florida. He grew up in a low-rent housing project, with his mother and four brothers and sisters. His father left the family when Ottis was eight years old. Doing her best to support five young children, Ottis's mother took a job as a motel maid. One son was killed in a tragic swimming accident just a few years later. Ottis became the leader of the "back of the projects gang," and was arrested while trying to steal some clothing from a shopping mall. "I still remember the whipping my mother gave me," he recalls. "She really beat me." Ottis turned his brush with the law into an inspiration on the high school football field. His heroics at West Palm Beach High School drew the attention of recruiters from the Universities of Notre Dame and Oklahoma. Determined to stay close to his family, however, he attended the University of Miami. There he found an important mentor in head coach Lou Saban. "I painted a much larger picture for him," says Saban. "I wanted him to know what a pro career could mean. It required harder work than he realized. And I told him it required dignity." The lesson in discipline took hold as Ottis completed his college degree program in Physical Education, and became the University of Miami's all-time leading rusher.

A college All-American in his senior season, Ottis was selected in the first round of the 1979 NFL Draft by the St. Louis Cardinals. In his first professional game, he rushed for 193 yards against a sturdy Dallas Cowboy defense. The precedent soon became a burden, however, as the St. Louis fans came

to accept nothing less. Still, he destroyed Earl Campbell's Rookie Rushing record (1,450) that season, averaging more than 100 yards per game. He was named the NFC's Rookie of the Year that season, and became the first rookie to win the league's Player of the Year Award.

When Super Bowl XXV arrived, Ottis was 34 years old and nearing the end of his career. His grinding 102-yard performance that day helped keep the powerful Buffalo Bills' offense off the field. Even so, the young Thurman Thomas piled up 135 yards on 15 carries of his own. When the Bills' Scott Norwood missed a last second field goal attempt wide right, Ottis was named the game's MVP. In football, sometimes the difference between a champion and another great running back can be a matter of inches!

PROFILE:
Ottis Anderson
Born: January 19, 1957
Height: 6' 2"
Weight: 220 pounds
Position: Running Back
College: University of Miami
Teams: St. Louis Cardinals (1979-1986) New York Giants (1986-1992)

Ottis Anderson makes a first down against the Seahawks.

1986-87
Super Bowl XXI
New York Giants (39) vs.
Denver Broncos (20)

1990-91
Super Bowl XXV
New York Giants (20) vs.
Buffalo Bills (19)

RAMPAGING ROOKIES

In the six year period between 1978 and 1983, the NFL's rookie record for rushing yardage was rewritten four times. In 1979, Ottis Anderson (1,605) supplanted Earl Campbell's record (1,450) set in the previous season. Two years later, George Rogers (1,674) surpassed Ottis. And in 1983, Eric Dickerson set the current mark (1,808).

TAKE A BREAK MA

Ottis remained close to his family throughout his college and professional career. As a rookie with the St. Louis Cardinals he would call his mother after every game. He later built a new house for her to live in, but she refused to give up her job as a maid. "She doesn't feel it's right not to work," Ottis said.

Ottis Anderson practicing with the University of Miami.

34

10,000 YARD CLUB

Ottis is one of ten players in NFL history to reach 10,000 yards rushing for his career. He is the all-time leading rusher in the franchise history of the Arizona Cardinals with 7,999 yards, and he gained an additional 2,274 with the Giants.

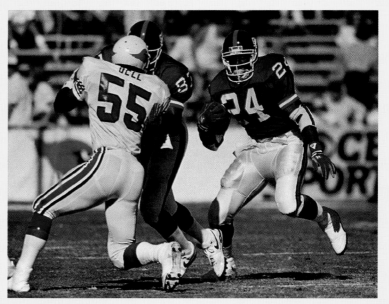

Ottis Anderson (24) running for the Giants.

NFL'S TOP 10 RUSHERS

Player	Carries	Yards	Avg.	long	TD
Walter Payton	3838	16726	4.4	76	110
Eric Dickerson	2996	13259	4.4	85	90
Tony Dorsett	2936	12739	4.3	99	77
Jim Brown	2359	12312	5.2	80	106
Franco Harris	2949	12120	4.1	75	91
John Riggins	2916	11352	3.9	66	104
O.J. Simpson	2404	11236	4.7	94	61
Marcus Allen*	2692	10908	4.1	61	103
Ottis Anderson	**2562**	**10273**	**4.0**	**76**	**81**
Barry Sanders*	2077	10172	4.9	85	73

*Active as of 1996

Marcus ALLEN

The average career of an NFL running back lasts about five seasons. Most will vanish from memory without making any impact on the all-time record book. Others exceed all expectations to become members of football's elite. Marcus Allen was the tenth player selected in the 1982 NFL Draft. Some said he was too small to be a fullback in the pros. Others thought he lacked the speed of a great halfback. What those scouts failed to measure was his desire to succeed.

Fifteen years later, Marcus Allen has played in more professional football games than any running back in history. As he closes out his illustrious career, he continues to climb the ladder of the all-time leader boards for Rushing Yards and TDs.

Marcus LeMarr Allen was born and raised in San Diego, California. He is one of five children born to Gwen and Harold "Red" Allen. According to Marcus, his parents taught him "to depend on no one," to be "proud and dignified," and to carry himself "as a winner." He grew up singing in the church choir, taking lessons on the piano, and playing basketball on the court his father had built in their back yard. He maintained strict study habits and regular attendance at Baptist Sunday school.

At San Diego's Lincoln High School, Marcus was a top performer on the basketball team until his sophomore season. Finding that his teammates did not share in his desire to win, he left the team and concentrated on his schoolwork. As a junior, Marcus became a star quarterback on the football team, and was equally as devastating on defense. He was a virtual one-man-team in his senior season, scoring four TDs on interception returns, passing for nine TDs, and running the ball for 12 more! Lincoln High School won the city championship

that season, and Marcus was named the best high school athlete in California.

Marcus had long been a fan of the University of Southern California Trojans. When he was recruited to play defensive back for the school's football team he didn't hesitate to accept the offer. In a surprise move, head coach John Robinson switched Marcus to the offensive backfield in his freshman season. While the decision shocked Robinson's coaching staff, it soon proved to be the correct assessment. Marcus spent his sophomore season as a blocking back for the Heisman Trophy winner, Charles White. In his final two seasons with the Trojans, Marcus became college football's leading all-purpose runner. As a senior, he took home a Heisman Trophy of his own.

The Los Angeles Raiders could not have been happier when nine teams passed on Marcus in the 1982 NFL Draft. Team officials stated he was their first choice from the beginning. Marcus proved them right by winning the AFC's Rookie of the Year Award. In his second season, he compiled the first of three straight 1,000-yard rushing

performances, and led the Raiders to victory in Super Bowl XVIII. Marcus was the MVP of the championship game, running for 191 yards and breaking the Super Bowl rushing record set by John Riggins (166 yards) the previous season.

As the years have passed, Marcus Allen has continued to produce award winning statistics. He was named the 1985 Player of the Year and MVP after leading the league in rushing (1,759), and tying Walter Payton's single-season record for nine straight 100-yard games. Marcus extended his streak to 11 games the next season, in setting the all-time career mark. In 1993, Marcus became a member of the Kansas City Chiefs where he broke Payton's all-time career record for rushing TDs in 1996.

PROFILE:
Marcus Allen
Born: March 26, 1960
Height: 6' 2"
Weight: 210 pounds
Position: Running Back
College: University of Southern California
Teams: Los Angeles Raiders (1982-1992), Kansas City Chiefs (1993-)

PORTRAIT OF A CHAMPION

CHAMPIONSHIP
SEASONS

Marcus Allen running for the Raiders.

1983-84
Super Bowl XVIII
Los Angeles Raiders (38) vs. Washington Redskins (9)

TROPHY CASE

1977–Hertz #1 Award–California's Best High School Athlete
1981–Heisman Trophy–College Football's Most Outstanding Player
1981–Maxwell Award–College Football's Most Outstanding Athlete
1982–AFC Rookie of the Year
1984–MVP, Super Bowl XVIII
1985–AFC Player of the Year
1985–NFL MVP Award

MAKE ROOM FOR MARCUS

The career of Marcus Allen continues to roll on. In 1996, he surpassed O. J. Simpson and John Riggins for career rushing yards, making him sixth on the all-time list. He also passed Walter Payton (110 TDs) to become the NFL's all-time leader for rushing TDs. When he finally hangs up his spikes there will be a spot reserved for him in the Professional Football Hall of Fame!

Marcus Allen with the Heisman Trophy.

REACH FOR THE STARS

Marcus credits his parents for giving him the will to succeed. He has disproved all doubters with his extraordinary ambition and self-confidence. "You've got to think positively to achieve the impossible, to be what you expect to be," he explains. "I have a burning desire to be the best. If I don't make it, that's O.K. because I'm reaching for something so astronomically high. If you reach for the moon and miss, you'll still be among the stars!"

Marcus Allen playing for the USC Trojans.

WHAT'S NEXT?

Marcus would like to be a television personality or broadcaster when his football career is over. In his spare time, he studies the martial art Tae Kwon Do and practices his footwork on the balance beam. He also enjoys playing piano and driving his Ferrari. He has played in more professional football games than any running back in history, and yet he considers football as "a great beginning" that "catapults you to other things."

Emmitt SMITH

Every generation of professional football fans has witnessed the exploits of a championship running back. In the 1920s, Red Grange and the Chicago Bears elevated the NFL to a level of popularity previously known only to the college game. In the 1940s, Marion Motley preceded Jim Brown as an unstoppable force in the backfield of the Cleveland Browns. Each champion's accomplishments are held up as a goal to be attained by the next generation's great star. Walter Payton is currently the NFL's all-time leading rusher. The man whose sights are firmly set on Walter's record is Emmitt Smith.

Emmitt J. Smith III is the oldest of six children born to Emmitt Jr. and Mary Smith. He was born in Pensacola, Florida. "There is nothing I am today that I would be without family," Emmitt says. His father was an outstanding high school athlete, who went on to play college basketball and semiprofessional football. He gave up his own attempts for a career in sports to care for his invalid mother. Emmitt's family placed the highest regard on the values of respect and discipline. He was never pressured by his father to play football, but was drawn to the game at a very young age.

At the age of five, Emmitt played touch football with his cousins. Two years later, he joined his first organized league. By the time he reached Brownsville Middle School, Emmitt was already a standout performer. He gained the immediate attention of the Escambia High School football coach, Dwight Thomas. Escambia's football team had suffered through nearly two decades of losing seasons. Thomas inserted Emmitt into the starting lineup as a freshman, and the team's fortunes quickly turned for the better. "For four years we did three things, and won two state championships doing them," Thomas said. "Hand the ball to Emmitt, pitch the ball to Emmitt, and throw the ball to Emmitt." In Emmitt's senior season, the Escambia High School football team was ranked number one in the nation.

Emmitt accepted a scholarship to the University of Florida, where he continued his incredible climb to the top. In the third game of his freshman season, he broke the school's single-game rushing record which had stood since 1930. In the seventh game, he surpassed the 1,000-yard rushing mark, attaining the milestone earlier than any player in collegiate football history! He was honored as college football's Freshman of the Year, and became only the second freshman ever to finish in the top 10 of the Heisman Trophy voting. After three seasons, Emmitt left the Gators to enter the NFL Draft. With one season of eligibility remaining, he already owned 58 school records!

The Dallas Cowboys were a team in transition when they drafted Emmitt Smith in 1990. Gone were long time head coach Tom Landry, and the glory days that earned them the title as "America's Team." In the six seasons since that time, Emmitt has won four NFL rushing titles, set an all-time record for TDs in a season (25), and led Dallas to three Super Bowl Championships. He has made the Cowboys "America's Team" once more, and made himself into a champion running back for a new generation of professional football fans to admire.

PROFILE:
Emmitt Smith
Born: May 15, 1969
Height: 5' 9"
Weight: 209 pounds
Position: Running Back
College: University of Florida
Teams: Dallas Cowboys (1990-)

CHAMPIONSHIP

SEASONS

Emmitt Smith waves to fans after a victory.

1992-93
Super Bowl XXVII
Dallas Cowboys (52) vs.
Buffalo Bills (17)

1993-94
Super Bowl XXVIII
Dallas Cowboys (30) vs.
Buffalo Bills (13)

1995-96
Super Bowl XXX
Dallas Cowboys (27) vs.
Pittsburgh Steelers (17)

JUST
PASSIN' BY

Emmitt Smith was passed by 16 teams in the 1990 NFL Draft. Many scouts felt he was too small to survive the professional ranks. The Dallas Cowboys had a different view of Emmitt as a player. They found he was a "hard worker" and "not a complainer." Since then, Emmitt has been one of the most durable running backs in the game, piling up 8,956 yards rushing in six seasons!

IN THE HUNT

A Comparison of the careers of Walter Payton and Emmitt Smith ...

Walter / through six seasons (1975-1980):

Attempts	Yards	TDs
1865	8386	65

Emmitt / through 6-seasons (1990-1995):

Attempts	Yards	TDs
2007	8956	96

Walter / Career (1975-1987):

Attempts	Yards	TDs
3838*	16726*	110*

*All NFL Records through 1995

AMERICA'S TEAM ONCE MORE

In the 1970s, the Dallas Cowboys appeared in five Super Bowls. By 1988, they had fallen to the bottom of the NFL standings. They finished with the league's worst record (1-15) for a second straight season after Jimmy Johnson replaced Tom Landry as head coach in 1989. Landry had been the head coach of Dallas since their first year in the league (1960). With the additions of Troy Aikman in 1989 and Emmitt Smith in 1990, the Cowboys quickly regained their status as "America's Team."

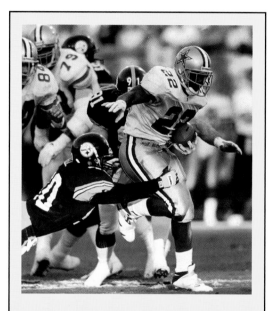

Emmitt Smith running for Dallas.

In 1993, Emmitt followed Walter Payton, Earl Campbell, and Jim Brown as only the fourth player to record three straight NFL rushing titles. He became the first member of the Dallas Cowboys to win the NFL's MVP Award. That same year Emmitt carried the Cowboys to its second straight NFL Championship. In Super Bowl XXVIII, Emmitt rushed for 132 yards and 2 TDs, and collected the Super Bowl MVP honors as well.

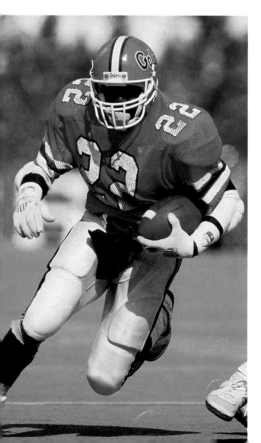

Emmitt Smith running for the University of Florida.

43

Glossary

AFC: The American Football Conference. One of two conferences in the NFL.

AFL: The American Football League (1960-1969). The AFL merged with the NFL in 1970, and after a slight reformation became the AFC.

All-American: A person chosen as the best amateur athlete at their position.

Contract: A written agreement a player signs when they are hired by a professional team.

Defense: The part of a team attempting to prevent the opposition from scoring.

Draft: A system in which new players are distributed to professional sports teams.

End Zone: The area at either end of the playing field between the goal line and the end line.

Freshman: A student in the first year of a U.S. high school or college.

Fullback: A running back named for his general positioning behind the offensive line. The fullback is usually the larger of the two running backs in the backfield.

Halfback: A running back named for his general position, (behind the quarterback and in front of the fullback) behind the offensive line.

Heisman Trophy: An award presented each year to the most outstanding college football player.

Interception: A pass in football that is caught by the opposition.

Junior: A student in the third year of a U.S. high school or college.

National Football League (NFL): The premier association of professional football teams, consisting of the American and National Football Conferences.

NCAA: National Collegiate Athletic Association. An organization that oversees the administration of college athletics.

NFC: The National Football Conference. One of two conferences in the NFL.

Offense: The part of a team that controls the ball and attempts to score.

Pass Reception: To catch (or receive) a thrown ball on offense.

Professional: A person who is paid for their work.

Quarterback: The player on a football team who leads the offense by controlling the distribution of the ball.

Running Back: The player on a football team whose main responsibility is to carry the ball, either by rushing or by pass reception.

Rushing: To move the ball by running.

Scholar-Athletes: An award given to collegians who excel in both athletics and classroom studies.

Senior: A student in the fourth year of a U.S. high school or college.

Sophomore: A student in the second year of a U.S. high school or college.

Super Bowl: The championship of the NFL, played between the American and National Conference Champions.

Touchdown: An act of carrying, receiving, or gaining possession of the ball across the opponent's goal line for a score of six points.

Varsity: The principal team representing a university, college, or school in sports, games, or other competitions.

Veteran: A player with more than one year of professional experience.

Index